P9-CKF-053

# A LITTLE
# SPOT
# OF ANXIETY

Written & Illustrated
by Diane Alber

To my children, Ryan and Anna:

Always remember that you have the power to CALM your ANXIETY SPOT down to a PEACEFUL SPOT!

Copyright © 2019 Diane Alber
All Rights Reserved
All inquiries about this book can be sent to the author at
info@dianealber.com
Published in the United States by Diane Alber Art LLC
ISBN: 978-1-951287-05-4
For more information, or to book an event, visit our website:
www.dianealber.com
Paperback
Printed in China

# This book belongs to:

_____

_____

_____

Hi! I'm a PEACEFUL SPOT!

And this GRAY SPOT is an ANXIETY SPOT.

Your **ANXIETY SPOT** can show up when you are feeling **worried, nervous, anxious, or scared.**

ANXIETY is one of the many emotions we can
experience every day. Other emotions are
SADNESS and ANGER, too!
We all have these emotions inside us.
But we feel the best when we are in our PEACEFUL SPOT.

Sadness          Anger          Anxiety

# Your ANXIETY SPOT makes you WORRY...A LOT!

Especially when you try new things.
Remember when you first tried to play soccer?

What if I am bad at this?

# Or when you had to take a test?

Every time your ANXIETY SPOT asks you
"What if...?" remember you can always answer
with, "I CAN DO THIS!"

That will help you change your
ANXIETY SPOT to a PEACEFUL SPOT, like me!

It's okay to have SMALL ANXIETY SPOTS because sometimes worrying protects you.
But when your WORRIES become TOO BIG or TOO MANY it doesn't feel very good. And it can make you miss out on things that are fun and good for you.

Sometimes when your ANXIETY begins to grow, it can cause a tummy ache or it can make you start to sweat. This is your body telling you that you need to manage your ANXIETY SPOT, QUICKLY!

Did you know there are things you can do that keep your ANXIETY SPOT from getting TOO BIG?

Like, making sure you are eating healthy!

And making sure you are getting plenty of rest!

This will give your body enough energy to help prevent your ANXIETY SPOT from showing up!

Music, drawing, and writing can help you express your worries through ART instead of letting your ANXIETY SPOT GROW!

Sometimes you end up in a situation where your ANXIETY SPOT surprises you!

And it can start growing really fast...
But before you panic, I want to show you how to

**QUICKLY** shrink your ANXIETY SPOT!

Okay, look at your hand...

Now imagine five GRAY SPOTS are on your fingers and one GREEN SPOT is on your palm.

Just like this!

Now with your pointer finger on your other hand, I want you to draw an imaginary line from one of the GRAY SPOTS, to the GREEN SPOT on your palm and repeat after me:

From the tip of my finger to the middle of my palm,

I can do this! I can be calm!

Imagine the worry on your GRAY SPOT (ANXIETY SPOT)
is traveling to the GREEN SPOT (PEACEFUL SPOT) and becoming CALM!

Now for the second part:

This worry grew too big, and cannot stay,

take a deep breath and blow it away!

Imagine yourself blowing the worry off of your GRAY SPOTS.
Now all you can see is a CALM GREEN SPOT!
Taking slow deep breaths is a great way to CALM your ANXIETY SPOT.
Now that it's not near you anymore, it can't make you worry!

Okay, now that you have learned a way to calm your ANXIETY SPOT down, let's try it in situations where your ANXIETY SPOT surprised you!

Like your first day of school...
Being away from your parents or guardian
can make you scared and anxious.

Or meeting new people can make you worried
that you won't fit in.

# This is a perfect time to practice our little trick!

From the tip of my finger to the middle of my palm,

# I can do this! I can be calm!

This worry grew too big, and cannot stay,

take a deep breath and blow it away!

Or when you showed up to a party, and your
**ANXIETY SPOT came with you!**

What if they don't like me?

Sometimes it's hard to be around new people. But worrying only makes your ANXIETY SPOT GROW! Instead...

Practice our little trick!

From the tip of my finger to the middle of my palm,

# I can do this! I can be calm!

This worry grew too big, and cannot stay,

take a deep breath and blow it away!

The more times that you can shrink your **ANXIETY SPOT** down, the stronger your **PEACEFUL SPOT** becomes!

Celebrate when you are able to
shrink down your ANXIETY SPOT! Use that confidence
to help you in new situations where your ANXIETY SPOT shows up!

If you need some help, just remember our little trick...

From the tip of my finger to the middle of my palm,

# I can do this! I can be calm!

This worry grew too big, and cannot stay,

take a deep breath and blow it away!

You can imagine your own spots or cut them out of construction paper and tape them to your fingers. You can also get real SPOT stickers in bulk on my website: www.dianealber.com